Penny's Poodle Puppy, Pickle

Penny's
Poodle Puppy,
Pickle

By Bernard Wiseman

GARRARD PUBLISHING COMPANY
CHAMPAIGN, ILLINOIS

*From Pickle
to Margaret Elizabeth's Schnauzers:
Mark, Elizabeth, Trinket,
Devon, Sandra, Clipper,
Pepita, and Chelsea*

Library of Congress Cataloging in Publication Data

Wiseman, Bernard.
 Penny's poodle puppy, Pickle

 SUMMARY: A poodle puppy named Pickle faces panic
at a picnic when he misunderstands everyone's desire to
"eat pickles."
 [1. Dogs—Fiction] I. Title.
PZ7.W7802Pe   [E]   79-26403
 ISBN 0-8116-6080-X

Penny's Poodle Puppy, Pickle

Penny got
a poodle puppy.
Penny named him
Pickle.

Penny took Pickle
to a picnic.
A lady said,
"I love
to eat PICKLES!"

So, Pickle ran away.

Penny yelled,
"Pickle! Pickle!
Come back, Pickle!

Pickle,

where ARE you?

Pickle!

Pickle?"

Penny cried,
"I can't find
my Pickle."
The lady said,
"Here—
eat one of
MY pickles."

Penny said,
"No, thank you.
I don't want
to eat a pickle."

The lady asked,
"Then why
do you want
YOUR pickle?"

Penny said,
"I want to
PAT my Pickle.

I want to
HUG my Pickle."

The lady said,
"You can pat
MY pickle—

And you can
hug MY pickle!"

"No!" Penny cried.
"I don't want
to pat or hug
YOUR pickle!

YOUR pickle
is a PICKLE.
MY Pickle is a PET."

The lady laughed.
"PICKLES cannot
be PETS."
Penny said,
"MY Pickle IS.
And he ran away.

My Pickle is
a poodle puppy.
You said
you love
to EAT PICKLES.
That made
my Pickle
run away."

The lady said,
"I will help you find
your Pickle.
Pickle! Pickle!
Where are you?"

Then the lady said,
"Let's look in
my picnic basket."
"Oh!" said Penny.
"My Pickle
is not in there!"

The lady said,
"I know. But
something else is . . ."

Penny yelled,

"Pickle! Pickle!

Here are HAMBURGERS!

Here are HOT DOGS!

Here are COOKIES!

Come and EAT!"

And Penny's
poodle puppy,
Pickle,
came running
back to Penny.